DOCTORS

BY EMMA LESS

AMICUS READERS ● AMICUS INK

Amicus Readers and Amicus Ink are imprints of Amicus
P.O. Box 1329, Mankato, MN 56002
www.amicuspublishing.us

Cataloging-in-Publication Data is on file with the Library of Congress.
ISBN 978-1-68151-293-8 (library binding)
ISBN 978-1-68152-275-3 (paperback)
ISBN 978-1-68151-355-3 (eBook)

Editor: Valerie Bodden
Designer: Patty Kelley

Photo Credits:
Cover: FatCamera/iStock
Inside: Dreamstime.com: Michael Zhang 3, Alexander Raths 7, Syda Productions 9, Wavebreakmedia 10, Petar Dojkic 13, Wessel du Plooy 15, Stephen McSweeny 16T, Stacy Barnett 16R, Dave Bredeson 16B. Shutterstock.com: Sirtravelalot 4.

Printed in China.

HC 10 9 8 7 6 5 4 3 2 1
PB 10 9 8 7 6 5 4 3 2 1

Doctors help us stay healthy.
The doctor is busy!

Doctors wash
their hands.
They do not want
to spread germs.

The doctor gives
Dan a check-up.
She listens
to his heart.

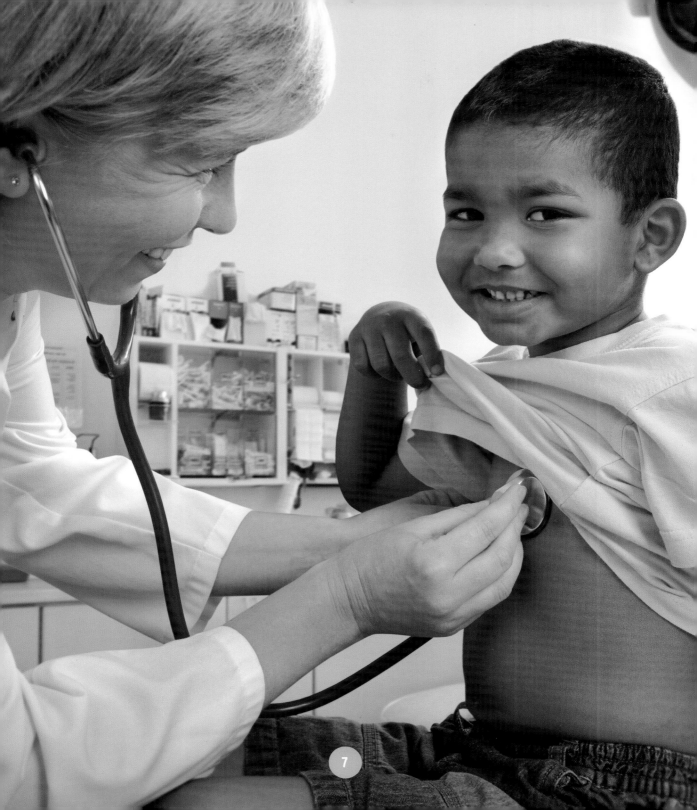

Noah listens to the doctor. She says to eat good food.

Jake is sick.
The doctor gives
him medicine.

Ouch! Don hurt his arm. The doctor puts on a cast.

Doctors keep people healthy. Maybe you will be a doctor!

SEEN IN A DOCTOR'S OFFICE

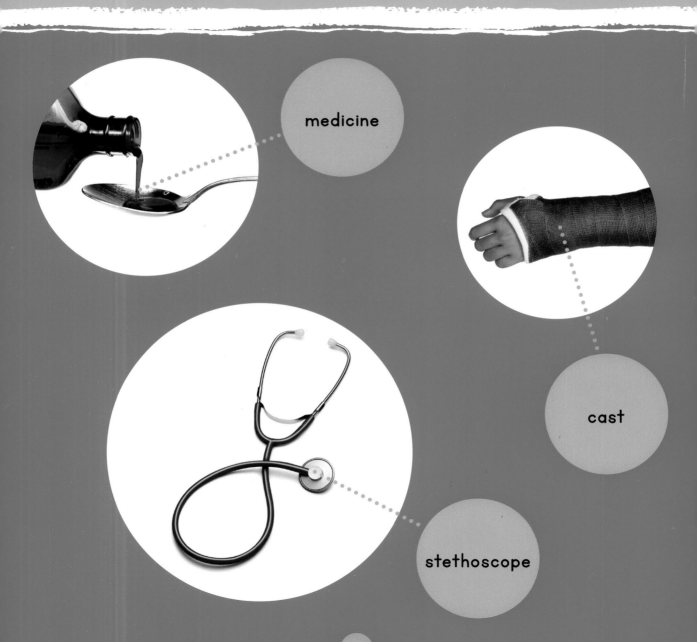

medicine

cast

stethoscope

16